EMERGENCY CHRISTMAS

EMERGENCY CHRISTMAS

JOHN L. LANSDALE

BookVoice Publishing 2018

Emergency Christmas Copyright © 2017
by John L. Lansdale
All rights reserved.

Design Copyright © 2017
by BookVoice Publishing
All rights reserved.

2018 Paperback Edition

ISBN
978-1-949381-01-6 Paperback
978-1-949381-00-9 eBook

BookVoice Publishing
PO Box 1528
Chandler, TX 75758
www.bookvoicepublishing.com

THE MECANA SERIES by John L. Lansdale
#1 - Horse of a Different Color
#2 - When the Night Bird Sings
#3 - Twisted Justice

Titles by John L. Lansdale
Slow Bullet
Long Walk Home
Zombie Gold
The Last Good Day
Broken Moon
Shadows West (with Joe R. Lansdale)
Hell's Bounty (with Joe R. Lansdale)
Boy and Hog (Short Story)
Boy and Hog Return (Short Story)
Emergency Christmas (Short Story)
Tales from the Crypt (Comic Series)
That Hellbound Train (Graphic Novel)
Yours Truly, Jack the Ripper (Graphic Novel)
Shadow Warrior (Graphic Novel)
Justin Case (Graphic Novel)

Follow the author online at
www.bookvoicepublishing.com
www.twitter.com/mybookvoice
www.goodreads.com/johnllansdale
www.facebook.com/bookvoicepublishing

What Others are Saying about John L. Lansdale

A "page-turner...Lansdale effectively delays revealing the novel's big secret until the end. Those who like their thrillers with a heavy dose of violent action will be satisfied."
- *Publishers Weekly* review of **Slow Bullet**

"This is an entertaining, science fiction-historical-horror blend with resourceful protagonists and a solid cast of secondary characters." – *Booklist* review of **Zombie Gold**

"The author's innate ability to spin a complex tale painted with vivid characters and intense suspense provides readers with a well-paced book that they may find difficult to set down...a worthwhile suspenseful ride."
- *Amazing Stories* review of **Horse of a Different Color**

"A straight-ahead thriller...it's about action, and there's plenty of that. Check it out."
- *Bill Crider's Pop Culture Magazine* review of **Slow Bullet**

"Has something for everyone... It's exciting, entertaining and educational. A fun ride."
- TV personality Joan Hallmark review of **Zombie Gold**

"Something unique and comfortable and difficult to put down. Highly recommended."
- *Cemetery Dance* review of **Hell's Bounty**

"True to Lansdale tradition, John L. Lansdale has compiled a piece of work that should appeal to a wide range of readers." – *Amazing Stories* review of **Zombie Gold**

Chapter 1

It was Christmas Eve and snow covered the windows, with a warning on the news of more to come.

Ashley Albright sat down her mug of hot chocolate and picked up the book she had been reading but couldn't really get into, not with her husband gone for the second Christmas in a row.

She put the book back on the end table and looked at the Christmas tree covered in twinkling lights with presents lying underneath.

The house lights flashed and went out for a moment before coming back on. It was bad enough to spend Christmas with out Kirk again, she thought, but now the power could go out, too.

The lights blinked again so she jumped up to retrieve a lantern and flashlight from the closet and then sat back down on the couch, placing both beside her and calling out for the kids.

"Mollie! Junior!" she yelled. "Get in here, it's getting dark and the lights may go out any minute."

They walked in from the kitchen.

Kirk Jr. looked a lot like his dad at ten years old, with his blonde hair and bright green eyes.

Mollie was twelve and was going to look just like her mother, still beautiful at thirty-eight. They had the same big blue eyes and infectious smiles that would brighten up the darkest day.

All the lights blinked again.

"If the lights go out we won't have Christmas tree lights and it won't seem like Christmas," Junior said.

"Not much of a Christmas, anyway, with Dad gone," Molly said.

"He'll be home next month. He would want us to enjoy Christmas, whatever happens," Ashley told them. "We have to call your grandparents tomorrow and wish them a Merry Christmas. And you better sound happy."

Ashley was a dutiful Army wife, but the holidays had always made her wish her husband could leave to spend more time with his family. He was just gone so much. As a Lt. Colonel with fifteen years in, at least he was getting closer to retirement, she told herself.

The doorbell rang.

"Who on earth could that be," Ashley said.

Junior started towards the door.

"Wait," Ashley said. "Let me get it, we're not expecting anyone."

Ashley walked to the door but snow outside had covered the peephole.

"Who's there?" she asked.

"Santa Clause," a familiar voice said.

"Oh my god," she said and swung open the door.

There stood her husband Kirk, with a duffle bag on his shoulder and a big smile on his face.

Ashley grabbed him around the neck. "I don't believe it," she said. "Why did you ring the bell?"

"I wanted to surprise you," he smiled.

"You did."

Snow was blowing on them through the open door. Kirk heard steps and looked up as Molly and Junior were running towards him. They both wrapped themselves around his legs.

"Can I come in?" he laughed as he tried to take a step.

Ashley grabbed him by the hand, pulled him away from the kids and snow, inside the house and closed the door. He dropped his bag and took Ashley in his arms, kissing her passionately then wrapping his arms around his kids.

"How did you get away?" Ashley said. "I wasn't expecting you until next month."

"My commander," he said. "He didn't want me missing another Christmas so he sent me home."

"It's going to be a great one now," Ashley said.

"All I need is you and the kids to make any Christmas great," he said.

"Well here we are," Ashley said. "We may have to welcome you in the dark. The lights keep flickering off and on. They may go out any minute."

"I'm looking forward to that," he took Ashley's hand and smiled.

A flash of light came from the Christmas tree and it caught fire.

Kirk ran and unplugged the tree. "Stay back," he said and started pitching the presents away from the tree.

The flames grew, and in a few seconds the tree was burning at a rapid rate. He grabbed a blanket off the couch and covered most of the tree and patted it down until the flames went out. He lifted the blanket off and smoke bellowed out. There was nothing left of the tree but burnt decorations and shriveled limbs. He carried the charred remains of the tree outside and left the door open for the smoke to escape.

"Dang, I wanted a Christmas tree," Junior said.

"We may not have one this year," Ashley said, "but I already got the present I wanted." She hugged Kirk and they fell onto the couch.

"Me too," Kirk said, looking into his wife's big, beautiful blue eyes.

"I don't care," Molly said. "Christmas is too much trouble anyway."

"Won't seem like Christmas without a Christmas tree," Junior said.

"I'll get you another one in the morning," Kirk said. "We'll open presents after that."

"Too late now, all the stores have sold out," Ashley said.

"Then I'll cut one down," he said.

"Where?" Ashley said. "There aren't any tree farms around here. And you'd have to drive ten miles in the snow just to even find any pine trees, and then probably get a fine for trespassing. Let's just forget it."

"Christmas is all show anyway," Molly said.

"We don't need a tree to celebrate Christmas," Ashley said.

"No, but Junior wants one. And I'm going to get one to make Christmas complete," Kirk said.

"Let's not worry about it anymore tonight," Ashley said. "I'm just happy you're home."

"Me too," Kirk said. "I love you so much. Nothing could be better than to come home for Christmas. I've got some gifts in my duffle bag but you'll have to wait until tomorrow."

"You know you shouldn't have said that," Ashley said. "The kids and I will find them. I put your present from last year in the garage, and was going to do the same with this year's, but you can have them tomorrow."

"From what you said, I think they're tools," he said. Ashley smiled as he bent over on the couch and picked her up. "You're my present."

"Kids, go to your rooms," Ashley said. "We'll see you in the morning."

They smiled and walked to their rooms.

Kirk carried Ashley to their bedroom.

Chapter 2

Everyone woke up early the next morning to Ashley fixing a Christmas breakfast.

Kirk walked in the kitchen with a big smile on his face. He hugged Ashley from behind and kissed her on the neck. "Merry Christmas," he said. "I'm not ever leaving again."

"You always say that, and then you have to leave," Ashley said.

"Not my choice," he said. "After breakfast I'm going to find a Christmas tree. I think I jinxed the other one."

"You don't have to do that," she said.

"Yes I do. Like Junior said, it's not Christmas without a tree."

"Well, we'll have to buy more decorations if you're going to get another tree."

"We'll all go. You and the kids can pick out the decorations."

Molly was the last one out the door with a sad look. "Do I have to go," she said.

"Yes," Ashley said. "Now get in the van."

"It's too cold and Dad's going to drive around the world to find a tree."

"Get in, we're not coming back until we find one," Kirk said.

"There's some pine trees about ten miles out of town in the forest park," Ashley said. "Did you bring an axe?"

"Yeah and sleeping bags, food and water. I'm a military man," he said. "I always prepare for everything. We'll find the perfect tree," he said.

"On someone else's property," Ashley joked. "If we can get there in this snow."

"It's not too bad. The snow's mostly stopped and the traffic is light."

"It's Christmas morning. You know, if you had been home longer I wouldn't let you do this."

"Humor me. I just got home, I want a tree to brag about."

Kirk backed the van out of the driveway and they headed to find a Christmas tree.

After ten miles on the highway, pine trees began to appear along the side of the road.

"There's some trees up ahead, Daddy, that look like Christmas trees," Junior said, pointing at a tree grove on the right side of the road.

"I see them," Kirk said. "We'll pull off the road. You all stay in the car. I'll take my axe and cut one down and we'll tie it on top of the van."

"Did you see the park sign," Ashley said. "The trees belong to the government."

"So do I," Kirk said.

"You may permanently if you cut down one of their trees," Ashley said.

An eighteen-wheeler was coming toward them and started sliding across the yellow line into their lane. The sound of his air breaks was like an airplane as he kept coming across the line in the snow.

Kirk accelerated to try and pass but the trailer jackedknifed as the back of it scraped the side of the van. He lost control for a second and slid off the side of the road, hitting a snow bank that spun them down an embankment. He slammed on the brakes but the van kept sliding down the hill, the snow getting deeper and deeper as they dodged tree after tree.

Kirk was able to turn the wheels just enough to miss a tree that would have caved in the front end of the van and possibly hurt someone.

Fortunately, the van came to a stop, a tree standing untouched by the right front fender.

"Anybody hurt?" Kirk asked.

"I'm alright," Molly said.

"Me too," Junior said.

"Ashley?"

"Banged my arm but it's okay," she said. "Scared me to death."

"I'm so sorry. That damn truck knocked us off the road." Kirk turned his head and looked back up the hill. "I bet it's half a mile back to the highway. Happened so fast I couldn't tell how far down the hill we came until we stopped."

He put the van in reverse but the snow was so thick the wheels couldn't turn.

"Looks like we're going to have to get some help to get out of here," he said. "We'll have to forget about the Christmas tree, I'm sorry to say."

"I'll call 911 to pick us up," Ashley said. "We can worry about the van later."

"Sorry," Kirk said.

"It's okay," Molly said from the back.

"Yeah, Dad, you were just trying to do something good," Junior added.

"Well, I won't say I told you so," Ashley grinned. "But it's okay, they'll come get us and we'll be home in time for Christmas."

Ashley took the phone out of her purse and dialed 911. The phone beeped and cut off. She dialed again and it did the same thing.

"Molly, give me your phone," she said and Molly handed her the phone. She dialed 911 again. Nothing - no sounds or rings.

"Mine's in my duffle bag," Kirk said.

"We must be in a dead spot here. Take the phone out of the car and see if you can get a signal," Ashley said and handed Kirk the phone.

He turned the door handle but the door wouldn't budge.

"The snow's piled up around us," Kirk said. "Let me try the window." He lowered the window, climbed out head-first into the snow and stood up, wiping off snow.

He dialed the phone. Nothing again.

"Give me your phone, Ashley," he said. She handed it to him out the window and he dialed 911. Still no signal.

The kids were getting frightened.

"What are we going to do, Daddy," Junior said. "We'll freeze."

"No you won't. It's going to be okay," Kirk said and looked at Ashley.

She knew that look meant there was a problem.

"Bound to be the location," Kirk said. "I'll move further out and try again."

"There are no houses out here," Molly said, looking across a field.

Kirk tried to walk in the snow but it was too deep. He started sinking like a rock every step he made.

He climbed back in the car through the window and wiped the snow off.

"We'll be okay," he reassured everyone.

"What are we going to do," Junior said.

"I'm going to cut off the van and save the heat for if we need it. Find a sleeping bag to get into if you get cold."

"So we're stuck here," Molly said.

"Kind of, but not for long," Kirk said.

"I don't like Christmas."

"It's not Christmas that did this, it was me and that truck."

"Speaking of the truck," Ashley said. "Tell them about it when you get through. We don't know what happened to him."

"I will," Kirk said.

"I see a deer standing by that big tree over there," Junior said.

"Is Santa Claus with him," Kirk joked.

"That's not funny," Ashley said.

"It is if you want it to be," Kirk said. "We're going to be alright. I came prepared." He picked up the phone and started dialing. "I'll try again."

This time it actually rang and a dispatcher came on the line.

"My name is Bill, how may I assist you," the man said.

Junior and Molly started yelling.

"Quiet!" Kirk said and spoke into the phone. "My name is Kirk Albright. I ran my van off an embankment close to the park sign on Highway 79 South. The snow's too deep to walk back to the highway."

Bill asked about their address, vehicle plate number, and tried to pinpoint their location. "Anyone else in the van?" he added.

"My wife and two kids. They're getting a little antsy," Kirk said. "When do you think they'll get here?"

"Responders are working as fast as possible, given the weather. Is anyone hurt?"

"No, not in the van. A truck jackknifed and ran us off the road," Kirk said. "We don't know what happened to him."

"We'll check on him, too. Do you have the van running?"

"Yes."

"How much fuel do you have, and do you have any blankets?" Bill asked.

"It's almost full," Kirk said. "I have sleeping bags and water and food for us all."

"That was good thinking in this weather," Bill said. "Make sure you don't have any fumes coming into the van, and only run it when it starts to get too cold. Responders will be there by morning. Please don't leave the van. If you have any problems, call us back."

"Roger that," Kirk said and handed the phone back to Ashley. "You heard him, they're coming, kids."

"We heard," Ashley said and smiled. "Want to snuggle?"

"Yeah," Kirk said and Ashley scooted over to him.

"Look, Dad, that tree in front of us looks like a Christmas tree," Junior said. "About the same size."

"Definitely would look like one if it had lights," Kirk said. "Wait a minute…we bought lights."

"So what," Molly said.

"I can hook them up to the van and save Christmas."

"How would you do that," Ashley said.

"My grandpa told me a true story about Christmastime when he was six and lived in a house with no electricity. He was sad about not having any Christmas lights. So his father, who was an auto mechanic, put lights on the tree and hooked them up to car batteries. And just like that, they had lights for Christmas. Grandpa said he never forgot that story. Maybe I can hook the lights up and we'll remember this Christmas as a good one, too."

"Do it!" Junior said. "That would be great, a lit-up Christmas tree in the wilderness."

"Then you'd really have a Christmas tree to remember," Kirk said. "Hand me that package of lights back there, Junior."

"I'm not sure that'll work," Molly said.

"We'll see," Kirk said as Junior handed him the package of lights.

He pulled the hood latch, started the van and climbed out the window with the lights. He pushed himself along the van to the back, dug out around the exhaust pipe and strung the lights on the tree that was no more than three feet away from the front fender. While shining his flashlight on the battery he hooked the lights to it, but nothing happened.

"Told you," Molly said, sticking her head out the window.

"I'm not done, yet, I'll figure it out," he said. "Put the windows up and keep it warm in there."

How in the hell did my great-granddad do this, Kirk thought to himself. He tried several combinations with the wires but nothing worked.

Kirk was ready to give up when he heard the sound of a limb breaking and the rustling of something in the trees. The noise got closer and he saw something moving toward him and he called out.

"Who's there," he said. No answer. "I hear you, who's there?"

Then he heard a voice.

"I saw your car lights and came to see if you were alright," the voice said. "Can I come on over?"

"Come on," Kirk said and took a tighter grip on his flashlight for a weapon if he needed it.

An elderly man with a slight limp, maybe in his seventies, walked in front of the car lights. He had a rough leathery-looking face with dark eyes. He was wearing a heavy red plaid coat and leather gloves. He had neatly-trimmed silver hair and was clean shaven. An unusual sight for where they were.

"Name's Bud," he said. "What happened here?"

"A truck ran me off the road. Help's on the way," Kirk said. "I was trying to hook up some Christmas lights on this tree to cheer up my family while we waited."

"Takes a special way to convert direct current to alternating current," Bud said, looking at the battery. "You have to bind them together to make it work."

"I know, my grandpa told me about his dad doing it for him on a Christmas tree when he was little, but nothing's happening for me."

"Let me borrow your flashlight and I'll see what I can do," Bud said and held out his hand for the light. "I'm a mechanic."

Kirk hesitated, thinking he might be trying to get it for a weapon, but after considering the difference between him and the old man he handed him the flashlight.

Bud pulled out a pocket knife, opened it, and shined the flashlight under the hood.

Ashley's window came down and she stuck her head out. "Who is that? What does he want?"

"He said he saw our lights and came to help. He thinks he can get the tree lights on," Kirk said.

"Tell him to come inside the van, it's too cold out there. You too," Ashley said.

Bud looked up from under the hood. "No thank you, ma'am, I'm fine."

Ashley put the window back up.

"Where did you come from," Kirk asked. "You live out here?"

"No, I was just passing through," Bud said.

"What do you mean passing through? The snow's too deep to walk in."

"I manage," he said and went back under the hood.

The lights on the tree came on and he rose up, handed the flashlight back to Kirk and stepped back.

"There you are, young man," he said. "Christmas tree lights."

"We'll, I'll be. It can be done," Kirk said.

"If you know how," Bud said. "Turn the headlights off and you can see the tree lights better."

The van lights went off and the tree lights seemed to glow brighter, lighting up the middle of nowhere.

A rear window went down and Junior stuck his head out. "They're great! Thanks, mister."

"You're welcome, son," Bud said.

Kirk made his way to the window and stuck his head inside. "See I told you. My grandpa wouldn't lie."

They were looking at Kirk, laughing.

"It is a special Christmas," Ashley said.

"Yeah, thanks to Bud," Kirk said. "I'm going to ask him to come with us to the house so we can thank him properly. It's something we'll all remember."

Kirk looked up from the van and saw the tree lights, but he didn't see Bud.

"Where'd he go," he asked. "Bud, where are you?"

No answer.

"Bud," he said again, still nothing. Kirk trudged around the tree and looked into the night but saw nothing. He yelled out again but there was no answer.

Bud was gone.

Ashley and the kids stuck their heads out the windows, yelling for Bud.

"Where did he go?" Ashley said.

"I don't know, he's disappeared."

"Where did he come from?" Ashley said.

"I don't know that, either. He said he was passing through," Kirk said.

"That's impossible," Ashley said.

"Why would he run off," Molly asked.

"I don't know," Kirk said. "I can't go looking for him. I'll tell the rescue squad when they get here. Maybe they can find him."

"He's going to freeze to death in this weather," Ashley said.

"Maybe they will be here soon to pick us up and can look for him," Kirk said. "Now put the windows up, I'm coming in. I'm freezing my butt off out here."

Kirk crawled in the window, raised it up and looked at the van's clock. "It will be daylight soon. Think I'll call again for Bud."

Chapter 3

A spotlight hit the van.

"They're here," Molly said.

"That's a relief," Ashley said.

"Can we take the tree with us?" Junior asked.

"Christmas is over now," Kirk said. "I'll unwire it. I want to see how Bud did it. You know, it was dark, but he reminded me of a picture I saw of my great-granddad with the same name."

"Don't you think you're getting a little bit carried away," Ashley said.

"Yeah, I guess so."

"They're coming down the hill on snowmobiles," Junior said with his head out the window.

The snowmobiles stopped behind the van. The responders got off and walked up to the van and Kirk let down the window.

A young man wearing a rescue uniform bent down to the window. His nametag read 'Fletcher.'

"Everybody alright in there?" Fletcher asked.

"We're okay," Kirk said.

"There's four of you, right?"

"Yes."

"Okay, we'll take two out at a time on the snowmobiles with us," Fletcher said. "You can call somebody for the van when the snow melts. Cut off the van and disconnect the tree lights. How in the world did you do that?'

"I didn't. An old man showed up and hooked it up for me. I guess he lives out here somewhere."

"Out here? No, this is park land. No one's allowed to live around here for miles. Maybe he came off the road."

"Don't think so, the snow's too deep. But he was here, hooked up those tree lights and disappeared. If you don't find him he'll die."

"He couldn't walk through the snow coming from the park land either," Fletcher said.

"I'm not lying. Even my family saw him."

"He was here," Ashley said.

"We saw him, too," Molly and Junior added.

"Alright, give me a description of the man and I'll turn it in. Best we can do is get a helicopter out here to look for him. What was his name?"

"He said it was Bud," Kirk said.

"What was the last name?"

"He didn't say, and I didn't think about asking him."

"Probably won't matter, if we see anyone it's probably him."

"Thanks," Kirk said.

"Okay, let's go," Fletcher said. "Kids, we'll take you first. Climb out the window. We'll be back to get you and your wife, next, Mr. Albright."

"Don't forget to get that helicopter out here," Kirk said. "He was a rugged-looking old man, maybe in his seventies, with silver hair, a kind smile and he said he was a mechanic. Had on a heavy red plaid coat. I owe him for a Christmas we'll always remember."

"He had long silvery hair and a beard?" Fletcher said. "Maybe it was Santa Claus."

"I'm serious. He had a regular hair cut and no beard," Kirk said. "Please find him."

"Okay," Fletcher said. "Let's get you out of here."

The kids climbed out the windows.

Kirk put up all the windows except the driver's-side one. "Come out my side," he told Ashley.

They each climbed out the window. He reached in and raised it as high as he could while still able to get his arm out.

He took one last look at the hook-up on the lights. "Man, that's all Greek to me," he said, scratching his head, and jerked the wires, the lights going out in a flash.

A little while later, the rescue squad dropped the Albrights off at their house and they went inside.

"What a day," Kirk said.

"It sure was," Ashley said. "We'll remember this Christmas for sure."

"I'm feeling a lot better about Christmas now," Molly said.

"Me too," Junior said.

"That's good," Kirk said.

"Count me in, too. What a night," Ashley said. "Let's get cleaned up, I have to be at work at three this afternoon. We'll open presents tonight. Kirk, you can take me to work in your truck and worry with the van later."

"I need a nurse's tender loving care," Kirk said.

"I'll get to you, big boy," Ashley said and gave him one of her super smiles.

"When you smile like that I just melt," he said.

"Well put yourself back together, we've got things to do," Ashley grinned.

"You go ahead," Kirk said. "I'll call a tow truck. Maybe they can get the van out today."

Ashley and the kids went to their rooms.

Kirk walked over to the coffee table, picked up the family photo album and thumbed through it until he came to a picture of his great-grandfather.

The picture was taken a year before he died, twenty years ago.

He was wearing a red plaid coat.

Kirk stared at the picture.

"It is him. And I'm the only one who would believe it."

He closed the album and placed it back on the coffee table.

The End

About the Author

John L. Lansdale was born and raised in East Texas. He is married to the love of his life Mary. They have four children. He is a retired Army reserve Psychological Operations Officer and a combat veteran with numerous medals and awards. Past roles include inventor, country music songwriter and performer, and television programmer. He produced and directed the Television Special "Ladies of Country Music." He has also produced several albums in Nashville, hosted his own radio shows and won awards for producing and writing radio and television commercials.

Lansdale was a writer and editor of a business newspaper. He has worked as a comic book writer for Tales from the Crypt, IDW, Grave Tales, Cemetery Dance and several more. He co-authored the Shadows West and Hell's Bounty novels with his brother Joe R. Lansdale. He is also the author of Zombie Gold, Horse of a Different Color, Slow Bullet, When the Night Bird Sings, Broken Moon, The Last Good Day, Long Walk Home and other titles coming soon.

THE MECANA SERIES by John L. Lansdale
#1 - Horse of a Different Color
#2 - When the Night Bird Sings
#3 - Twisted Justice

Titles by John L. Lansdale
Slow Bullet
Long Walk Home
Zombie Gold
The Last Good Day
Broken Moon
Shadows West (with Joe R. Lansdale)
Hell's Bounty (with Joe R. Lansdale)
Boy and Hog (Short Story)
Boy and Hog Return (Short Story)
Emergency Christmas (Short Story)
Tales from the Crypt (Comic Series)
That Hellbound Train (Graphic Novel)
Yours Truly, Jack the Ripper (Graphic Novel)
Shadow Warrior (Graphic Novel)
Justin Case (Graphic Novel)

SLOW BULLET
by John L. Lansdale

A "page-turner... Those who like their thrillers with a heavy dose of violent action will be satisfied." - *Publishers Weekly*

In this timely novel, Clark McKay, a retired Army Special Forces Colonel, has developed a drinking problem after losing his wife and son in a car accident, as well as from the nightmares of his Vietnam days. And he's not getting any younger. In spite of his problems, he is determined to find out who murdered his best friend and his friend's wife.

A Washington D.C. detective refuses to believe McKay has found the murderer, a former CIA operative and arms dealer who murdered McKay's friend because he discovered the truth behind the assassination of JFK – preventing President John F. Kennedy from ending the Vietnam War.

McKay learns there are CIA documents his friend hid that will prove the conspiracy to be true. His search for these documents takes him all over the world. On his journey, after wading through all the corruption, McKay is brought to the conclusion that he may have to resort to murder if justice is to be served.

What happened over fifty years ago is still with us today. In fact, many still doubt the "lone gunman" theory put forth by the Warren Commission. Could there truly have been a conspiracy to keep JFK from ending the war?

Truth and fiction make an interesting mixture in this fast-paced and entertaining novel. There are always those who escape justice. One hand washes the other, unless you have someone like Clark McKay who is willing to pay the ultimate price.

A "straight-ahead thriller...it's about action, and there's plenty of that. Check it out." – *Bill Crider's Pop Culture Magazine*

HORSE OF A DIFFERENT COLOR
a Mecana Novel
by John L. Lansdale

Someone is murdering and mutilating young women in a Dallas suburb, using the same techniques as a case down in Houston the previous year.

When the second body is found, it seems the killer has moved his hunting grounds to the Dallas area.

As the body count rises, Detective Thomas Mecana – a divorced fifteen-year veteran of the Dallas Police Department – is assigned to the case.

He prides himself on always getting his man, but his tried-and-true methods of the past are not working.

To make matters worse, his supervisor assigns him a new partner, a young officer who has never before worked a murder case.

Add in two teenage daughters creating problems at home, and a boss threatening to fire him at work, and Mecana's life begins to unravel as he hones in on his suspect.

With hard work, and some luck, Mecana and his partner discover a most-unusual serial killer case with murder in its very genes.

They discover some evidence is so strange and unbelievable, it might be best left alone.

Checkmate.

"…the author's innate ability to spin a complex tale painted with vivid characters and intense suspense provides readers with a well-paced book that they may find difficult to set down."
– Ricky L. Brown, *Amazing Stories*

WHEN THE NIGHT BIRD SINGS
a Mecana Novella
by John L. Lansdale

Mecana is back in this follow-up to Horse of a Different Color.

Shortly after solving the horrific Mutilator serial killer case, detectives Thomas Mecana and Darcie Connors are on the trail of a new suspect.

On the inaugural day of their own private investigation firm, the two detectives meet Candy Kane - a lascivious Dallas socialite who offers them a small fortune in exchange for protection.

A former patient of her psychotherapist husband has been trying to settle old scores by threatening Mrs. Kane' life.

And he's not the only one out for vengeance.

With an ever-growing suspect list, Mecana must toe the line between friend and foe.

Each action leaves them sitting in the crosshairs of those wanting to claim the Kane fortune.

One wrong move could mean the end.

TWISTED JUSTICE
a Mecana Novella
by John L. Lansdale

Newlywed private detectives Thomas Mecana and Darcie Connors have barely shaken their honeymoon jetlag before taking on another case in the Lone Star State.

Dallas Homicide Detective Sunday Verves is looking into the suspicious deaths of local drug runners when she discovers a potential suspect that hits too close to home – Angela, the daughter of her superior officer, and Angela's lawyer boyfriend.

When the trail leads her south of the border, Verves enlists her old friend Mecana and his new wife into tracking down Angela and her boyfriend.

What they discover down Mexico way turns the case on its head and sends the group searching for clues to a bigger piece of the puzzle.

Ultimately, Sunday Verves finds she must choose between avenging wrongs of the past or righting wrongs of the present.

Sometimes the only choice is TWISTED JUSTICE.

LONG WALK HOME
a novel by
John L. Lansdale

Ten-year-old Trenton O'Rourke's life was changed forever during the summer of 1944. He and his family lived on a fading farm like many others in the small town of Angel Point, Mississippi. With family members fighting in World War II overseas, and rising racial tensions back home, what was normally a routine summer turned into a nightmare of murder, loss, trying to cope with hard times to survive and surprise learning experiences of growing up. Trenton's life would have never been what it was had it not been for a chance encounter with someone nobody expected.

Keep your eyes peeled for

THE LAST GOOD DAY
by John L. Lansdale

and

BROKEN MOON
by John L. Lansdale

Two new Westerns from
John L. Lansdale and BookVoice Publishing

STAY CONNECTED WITH BOOKVOICE AND JOHN L. LANSDALE

Follow us online at
www.bvpstore.com
www.bookvoicepublishing.com
www.twitter.com/mybookvoice
www.goodreads.com/johnllansdale
www.facebook.com/bookvoicepublishing

BookVoice
Publishing

www.ingramcontent.com/pod-product-compliance
Lightning Source LLC
Chambersburg PA
CBHW051829180726
48283CB00004BA/1362